David Garrick, Michael Arne

Cymon

a dramatic romance

David Garrick, Michael Arne

Cymon
a dramatic romance

ISBN/EAN: 9783337382612

Printed in Europe, USA, Canada, Australia, Japan

Cover: Foto ©Andreas Hilbeck / pixelio.de

More available books at **www.hansebooks.com**

A

DRAMATIC ROMANCE.

As it is Performed at the

THEATRE-ROYAL in Drury-Lane.

The MUSIC by Mr. ARNE.

——————Soli cantari periti
ARCADES.

A NEW EDITION.

L O N D O N,

Printed for T. Becket and P. A. De Hondt, in
the Strand. MDCCLXX.

PROLOGUE,

For New Year's Day.

Spoken by Mr. KING.

I Come, obedient at my Brethren's Call,
  From Top to Bottom, to salute you all;
Warmly to wish, before our Piece you view,
A happy Year—to you—you—you—and you!
        Box'—Pit—1 Gall^y—2 Gall^y.
From you the Play'rs enjoy and feel it here,
The merry Christmas, and the happy Year.
  There is a good old Saying—pray attend it;
As you begin the Year, you'll surely end it.
Should any one this Night incline to Evil,
He'll play for twelve long Months, the very Devil!
Should any married Dame exert her Tongue,
She'll sing the Zodiac round, the same sweet Song:
And should the Husband join his Music too,
Why then 'tis Cat and Dog, the whole Year thro'.
Ye Sons of Law and Physic, for your Ease,
Be sure this Day you never take your Fees:
Can't you refuse?—Then the Disease grows strong,
You'll have two Itching Palms—Lord knows how
    long!
Writers of News by this strange Fate are bound,
They fib To-day, and fib the whole Year round.
You Wits assembled here, both great and small,
Set not this Night afloat your Critic Gall;
If you should snarl, and not incline to Laughter,
What sweet Companions for a Twelvemonth after!
You must be muzzled for this Night at least;
Our Author has a Right this Day to feast.
He has not touch'd one Bit as yet.—Remember,
'Tis a long Fast from now to next December.

'Tis

'Tis Holiday! *you are* our Patrons *now*;
     (to the upper Gallery.
If you but grin, the Critics won't Bow, wow.
As for the Plot, Wit, *Humour, Language—I*
Beg you such Trifles kindly to pass by;
The most essential Part, which something means,
As Dresses, Dances, Sinkings, Flyings, Scenes,—
They'll make you stare—nay, there is such a thing,
Will make you stare still more!—for I must sing:
And should your Taste, and Ears, be over nice,
Alas! you'll spoil my Singing in a Trice.
If you should growl, *my Notes will alter soon,*
I can't be in—if you are out *of Tune!*
Permit my Fears your Favour to bespeak,
My Part's a strong one, and poor I *but weak.*
    (alluding to his late Accident.
If you but smile, I'm firm, if frown, I stumble—
Scarce well of one, *spare me a* second *Tumble!*

Dramatis Personæ.

MERLIN,	Mr. BENSLEY.
CYMON,	Mr. VERNON.
DORUS,	Mr. PARSONS.
LINCO,	Mr. KING.
DAMON,	Mr. FAWCETT.
DORILAS,	Mr. FOX.
HYMEN,	· Mr. GIORGI.
CUPID, ·	Miss ROGERS.

Demons of Revenge, Mr. CHAMPNESS, &c. &c.

Knights, Shepherds, &c. &c. &c. &c.

URGANDA,	Mrs. BADDELEY.
SYLVIA,	Mrs. ARNE.
FATIMA,	Mrs. ABINGTON.
First SHEPHERDESS,	Miss REYNOLDS.
Second SHEPHERDESS,	Miss PLYM.
DORCAS,	Mrs. BRADSHAW.

SCENE, ARCADIA.

C Y M O N.

A

DRAMATIC ROMANCE.

ACT I.

SCENE, URGANDA's *Palace.*

Enter MERLIN *and* URGANDA.

URGANDA.

BUT hear me, Merlin, I befeech you, hear me.

MERLIN.

Hear you! I have heard you—for years have heard your vows, your proteftations—Have you not allur'd my affections by every female art? and when I thought that my unalterable paffion was to be rewarded for its conftancy—What have you done?—Why, like mere mortal woman, in the true fpirit of frailty, have given up me and my hopes—for what? a boy, an ideot.

B

URGANDA.

Ev'n this I can bear from Merlin.

MERLIN.

You have injur'd me, and muſt bear more.

URGANDA.

I'll repair that injury.

MERLIN.

Then ſend back your fav'rite Cymon to his diſconſolate friends.

URGANDA.

How can you imagine that ſuch a poor igno-rant object as Cymon is can have any charms for me?

MERLIN.

Ignorance, no more than profligacy, is ex-cluded from female favour; the ſucceſs of rakes and fools, is a ſufficient warning to us, could we be wiſe enough to take it.

URGANDA.

You miſtake me, Merlin; pity for Cymon's ſtate of mind, and friendſhip for his father, have induc'd me to endeavour at his cure.

MERLIN.

Falſe, prevaricating Urganda! Love was your inducement. Have you not ſtolen the prince from his royal father, and detained him here by your power, while a hundred knights are in ſearch after him? Does not every thing about you prove the conſequence of your want of ho-nour and faith to me? Were you not plac'd on this happy ſpot of Arcadia, to be the guardian of its peace and innocence? and have not the

Arcadians

Arcadians liv'd for ages the envy of lefs happy, becaufe lefs virtuous people?

U R G A N D A.

Let me befeech you, Merlin, fpare my fhame.

M E R L I N.

And are they not at laft, by your example, funk from the ftate of happinefs and tranquillity to that of care, vice, and folly! Their once happy lives are now imbitter'd with envy, paffion, vanity, felfifhnefs, and inconftancy;—and who are they to curfe for this change? Urganda, the loft Urganda.

A I R.

If pure are the fprings of the fountain,
  As purely the river will flow,
If noxious the ftream from the mountain,
  It poifons the valley below:
    So of vice, or of virtue, poffeft,
      The throne makes the nation,
      Thro' ev'ry gradation,
    Or wretched, or bleft.

Omitted in the reprefentation.

U R G A N D A.

Let us talk calmly of this matter.

M E R L I N.

I'll converfe with you no more—becaufe I will be no more deceiv'd: I cannot hate you, tho' I fhun you—Yet, in my mifery, I have this confolation, that the pangs of my jealoufy are at leaft equall'd by the torments of your fruitlefs paffion.

Still wifh and figh, and wifh again,
LOVE is dethron'd, REVENGE fhall reign!
Still fhall my pow'r your arts confound,
AND CYMON'S CURE SHALL BE URGANDA'S
    WOUND.   [*Exit* Merlin.

URGANDA.

" *And* Cymon's *cure fhall be* Urganda's
wound!" What myftery is couch'd in thefe
words?—What can he mean?

Enter Fatima, *looking after* Merlin.

FATIMA.

I'll tell you, madam, when he is out of hearing—He means mifchief, and terrible mifchief
too; no lefs, I believe, than ravifhing you, and
cutting my tongue out—I wifh we were out of
his clutches.

URGANDA.

Don't fear, Fatima.

FATIMA.

I can't help it, he has great power, and is mif-
chievoufly angry.

URGANDA.

Here is your protection, (*fhewing her wand.*)
My power is at leaft equal to his—(*mufes.*) " *And*
Cymon's *cure fhall be* Urganda's *wound!*"

FATIMA.

Don't trouble your head with thefe odd erds
of ver es, which were fpoke in a paffion; or,
perhaps, for the rhyme's fake.—Think a little
to clear us from this old mifchief-making con-
jurer—What will you do, madam?

U R G A N D A.

What can I do, Fatima?

F A T I M A.

You might very eafily fettle matters with him, if you cou'd as eafily fettle 'em with your-felf.

U R G A N D A.

Tell me how?

F A T I M A.

Marry Merlin, and fend away the young fel-low. (*Urganda fhakes her head.*) I thought fo—we are all alike, and that folly of ours of pre-ferring two-and-twenty to two-and-forty, runs thro' the whole fex of us—but, before matters grow worfe, give me leave to reafon a little with you, madam.

U R G A N D A.

I am in love, Fatima (*fighing.*)

F A T I M A.

And poor reafon may ftay at home—me ex-actly!—Ay, ay, we are all alike—but with this difference, madam—your paffion is furely a ftrange one—you have ftolen away this young man; who, bating his youth and figure, has not one fingle circumftance to create affection about him: He is half an ideot, madam, which is no great compliment to your wifdom, your beauty, or your power.

U R G A N D A.

I defpife them all -- for they can neither relieve my paffion, or create one where I would have them.

       A I R.

A I R.

What is knowledge, and beauty, and power,
Or what is my magical art ?
Can I for a day, for an hour,
Have beauty to make the youth kind,
Have pow'r o'er his mind,
Or knowledge to warm his cold heart :
O! no—a weak boy all my magic disarms,
And I sigh all the day with my power and my charms.

F A T I M A.

Sigh all the day !---More shame for you, madam—Cymon is incapable of being touch'd with any thing; nothing gives him pleasure, but twirling his cap, and hunting butterflies—he'll make a sad lover indeed, madam—

U R G A N D A.

I can wait with patience for the recovery of his understanding; it begins to dawn already.

F A T I M A.

Where pray ?

U R G A N D A.

In his eyes.

F A T I M A.

Eyes !—Ha, ha, ha, ha!—Love has none, madam—the heart only sees, on these occasions—Cymon was born a fool—and his eyes will never look as you would have them, take my word for it.

U R G A N D A.

Don't make me despair, Fatima.

FATIMA.

F A T I M A.

Don't lose your time then; 'tis the businefs of beauty to make fools, and not cure 'em—Even I, poor I, could have made twenty fools of wife men, in half the time that you have been endeavouring to make your fool fensible— O! 'tis a fad way of spending one's time.

U R G A N D A.

Hold your tongue, Fatima—my passion is too serious to be jested with.

F A T I M A.

Far gone indeed, madam—and yonder goes the precious object of it. *(looking out.*

U R G A N D A.

He seems melancholy: what's the matter with him?

F A T I M A.

He's a fool, or he might make himself very merry among us—I'll leave you to make the most of him.

U R G A N D A.

Stay, Fatima—and help me to divert him.

F A T I M A.

A fad time, when a lady must call in help to divert her gallant!—but I'm at your fervice.—

U R G A N D A.

A I R.

Hither, all my spirits, bend,
With your magic powers attend,
  Chafe the mists that cloud his mind:
Musick, melt the frozen boy,
Raife his foul to love and joy;
  Dulnefs makes the heart unkind.

Enter

Enter Cymon *melancholy.*

C Y M O N.

What do you fing for ?—Heigho ! (*fighing.*

F A T I M A.

What's the matter, young gentleman ?

C Y M O N.

Heigho !

U R G A N D A.

Are you not well, Cymon ?

C Y M O N.

Yes,—I am very well.

U R G A N D A.

Why do you figh then ?

C Y M O N.

Eh ! (*looks foolifhly.*)

F A T I M A.

Do you fee it in his eyes, now, madam ?

U R G A N D A.

Prithee, be quiet—What is it you want ? tell me, Cymon—Tell me your wifhes, and you fhall have 'em.

C Y M O N.

Shall I ?

U R G A N D A.

Yes indeed, Cymon.

F A T I M A.

Now, for it.

C Y M O N.

I wifh—heigho !

URGAN-

U R G A N D A.

These sighs must mean something.

(aside to Fatima.)

F A T I M A.

I wish you joy then; find it out, madam.

U R G A N D A.

What do you sigh for?

C Y M O N.

I want——   (sighs.)

U R G A N D A.

What, what, my sweet creature?   (eagerly.)

C Y M O N.

To go away.

F A T I M A.

O la!—the meaning's out.

U R G A N D A.

What would you leave me then?

C Y M O N.

Yes.

U R G A N D A.

Why would you leave me?

C Y M O N.

I don't know.

U R G A N D A.

Where would you go?

C Y M O N.

Any where.

U R G A N D A.

Had you rather go any where, than stay with me?

C

CYMON.

I had rather go any where, than ſtay with any
body.

URGANDA.

But you can't love me, if you would leave me,
Cymon.

CYMON.

Love you! what's that.

URGANDA.

Do you feel nothing here? In your heart,
Cymon?

CYMON.

Yes, I do.

URGANDA.

What is it?

CYMON.

I don't know.   (ſighs.)

URGANDA.

That's a ſigh, Cymon—am I the cauſe of it?

CYMON.

Yes, indeed you are.

URGANDA.

Then I am bleſt!

FATIMA.

Poor lady!

URGANDA.

But how do I cauſe it?

CYMON.

You won't let me go away.

FATIMA.

Poor lady!   (aſide.)

URGANDA.

U R G A N D A.

Will you love me, If I let you go ?

C Y M O N.

Any thing, if you'll let me go—pray let me go.

U R G A N D A.

You can't love me, and go too.

C Y M O N.

Let me try.

F A T I M A.

I'm out of all patience—what the deuce would you have, young gentleman ? Had you one grain of underſtanding, or a ſpark of ſenſibility in you, you would know and feel yourſelf to be the happieſt of mortals.

C Y M O N.

I had rather go, for all that.

F A T I M A.

The picture of the whole ſex ! Oh ! madam —fondneſs will never do, a little coquetry is the thing ; I bait my hook with nothing elſe ; and I always catch fiſh.   (*aſide to* Urganda.)

U R G A N D A.

What ! had you rather go away than live here in ſplendor, be careſs'd by me, and have all your commands obey'd ?

C Y M O N.

All my commands obey'd ?

U R G A N D A.

Yes, my dear Cymon ; give me your affections, and I will give you my power—you ſhall be lord of me and mine.

C 2   CYMON.

C Y M O N.

O la!

F A T I M A.

O, the fool!

U R G A N D A.

I will shew him my power, and captivate his
heart thro' his senses.

F A T I M A.

You'll throw away your powder and shot.

Urganda *waves her wand, and the stage changes to
a magnificent garden.* Cupid *and the* Loves *descend.*

C U P I D.

A I R.

O! why will you call me again,
　'Tis in vain, 'tis in vain;
　　The pow'rs of a god
　　Cannot quicken this clod,
　Alas!—It is labour in vain:
O Venus my mother, some new object give her!
This blunts all my arrows, and empties my quiver.

A dance by Cupid *and followers.*

During the entertainments of Singing and Dancing,
　Cymon *at first stares about him, then grows in-
attentive, and at last falls asleep.*

U R G A N D A.

Look, Fatima, nothing can affect his insensi-
bility—and yet, what a beautiful simplicity!

F A T I M A.

F A T I M A.

Turn him out among the fheep, madam, and think no more of him—'Tis all labour in vain, as the fong fays, I affure you.

U R G A N D A.

Cymon, Cymon! what are you dead to thefe entertainments?

C Y M O N.

Dead! I hope not.   (*ftarts.*)

U R G A N D A.

How can you be fo unmov'd?

C Y M O N.

They tir'd me fo, that I wifh'd 'em a good night, and went to fleep—But where are they?

U R G A N D A.

They are gone, Cymon.

C Y M O N.

Then let me go too.   (*going.*)

F A T I M A.

The old ftory!   *

U R G A N D A.

Whither would you go?—Tell me, and I'll go with you, my fweet youth.

C Y M O N.

No, I'll go by myfelf.

U R G A N D A.

And fo you fhall; but where?

C Y M O N.

Into the fields.

URGANDA.

But is not this garden pleafanter than the
fields, my palace than cottages, and my com-
pany more agreeable to you than the fhepherds?

CYMON.

Why how can I tell till I try; you won't let
me chufe.

A I R.

You gave me laft week a young linnet.
Shut up in a fine golden cage;
Yet how fad the poor thing was within it,
Oh how did it flutter and rage!
Then he mop'd, and he pin'd,
That his wings were confin'd,
Till I open'd the door of his den;
Then fo merry was he,
And becaufe he was free,
He came to his cage back again.

And fo fhould I too, if you would let me go.

URGANDA.

And would you return to me again?

CYMON.

Yes I would—I have no where elfe to go.

FATIMA.

Let him have his humour—when he is not
confin'd, and is feemingly difregarded, you may
have him, and mould him as you pleafe.—'Tis
a receipt for the whole fex.

URGANDA.

I'll follow your advice—Well, Cymon, you
fhall go wherever you pleafe, and for as long as
you pleafe.

CYMON.

C Y M O N.

O la! and I'll bring you a bird's neft, and
fome cowflips—and fhall I let my linnet out
too?

F A T I M A.

O, ay, pretty creatures; pray, let 'em go
together.

U R G A N D A.

And take this, Cymon, wear it for my fake,
and don't forget me. (*Gives* Cymon *a nofegay.*)
Tho' it won't give paffion, it will encreafe it,
if he fhould think kindly of me, and abfence
may befriend me (*Afide.*) Go, Cymon, take
your companion, and be happer than I can
make you.

C Y M O N.

Then I'm out of my cage, and fhall mope
no longer. (*overjoyed.*)

U R G A N D A.

His tranfports diftract me!—I muft retire
to conceal my uneafinefs.   (*Retires.*)

F A T I M A.

And I'll open the gate to the prifoners. [*Exit.*

C Y M O N.

And I'll fetch my bird, and we'll fly away together.

A I R.

A I R.

Oh liberty, liberty !
Dear happy liberty !
  Nothing's like thee !
  So merry are we,
My linnet and I,
  From prison we're free,
Away we will fly,
  To liberty, liberty,
  Dear happy liberty !
Nothing's like thee !

END *of the* FIRST ACT.

A C T II.

SCENE, *A Rural Prospect.*

Enter two Shepherdesses.

FIRST SHEPHERDESS.

WHAT to be left and forsaken! and see the false fellow make the same vows to another, almost before my face! I can't bear it, and I won't!

SECOND SHEPERDESS.

Why, look ye, Sister, I am as little inclin'd to bear these things as yourself; and if my swain had been faithless too, I should have been vex'd at it, to be sure; but how can you help yourself?

FIRST SHEPHERDESS.

I have not thought of that; I only feel I can't bear it; and as to the *won't*, I must trust in a little mischief of my own to bring it about.— O, that I had the power of our enchantress yon‚ der! I wou'd play the devil with them all.

SECOND SHEPHERDESS.

And yet folks say, she has no power in love-matters; you know, notwithstanding her charms, and her spirits, she is in love with a fool, and has not wit enough to make him return it.

D   FIRST

FIRST SHEPERDESS.

No matter for that; if I could not make folks love me, I would make them miferable, and that's the next pleafure to it.

SECOND SHEPHERDESS.

And yet, to do juftice to her who makes all this difturbance among you, fhe does not in the leaft encourage the fhepherds, and fhe can't help their falling in love with her.

FIRST SHEPHERDESS.

May be fo, nor can I help hating and deteft-ing her, becaufe they do fall in love with her.— Sylvia's good qualities cannot excufe her to me; my quarrel to her is, that all the young fellows follow her, not becaufe fhe does not follow the young fellows.

SECOND SHEPHERDESS.

Well, but really now, fifter, 'tis a little hard, that a girl, who has beauty to get lovers, or merit enough to keep 'em, fhould be hated for her good qualities. (*Affectedly.*)

FIRST SHEPHERDESS.

Marry come up, my infulting fifter; becaufe you think your fhepherd conftant, you have no feeling for the falfe-heartednefs of mine.—But don't be too vain with your fuccefs; my Dori-las is made of the fame ftuff as your Damon; and I can't for the life of me fee that you have any particular fecurity for your fool, more than I had for mine.

SECOND SHEPHERDESS.

Why are you fo angry, my dear fifter?—I am not Sylvia, and to oblige you, I will abufe her wherever I go, and whenever you pleafe; I think fhe is a moft provoking creature, and I

wifh

wifh fhe was out of the country with all my foul.

FIRST SHEPHERDESS.

And fo fhe ought to be. She has no bufinefs here with her good qualities. Nobody knows who fhe is, or whence fhe came.—She was left here with old Dorcas; but how, or by whom, or for what, except to make mifchief among us, I know not—There is fome myftery about her, and I'll find it out.

SECOND SHEPHERDESS.

But will your quarrelling with her bring back your fweetheart?

FIRST SHEPHERDESS.

No matter for that—when the heart is over-loaded, any vent is a relief to it; and that of the tongue is always the readieft and moft natural —So if you won't help me to find her, you may ftay where you will.

LINCO, *finging without.*
Care flies from the lad that is merry.

SECOND SHEPHERDESS.

Here comes the merry Linco, who never knew care, or felt forrow.—If you can bear his laughing at your griefs, or finging away his own, you may get fome information from him.

Enter Linco *finging.*

LINCO.

What, my girls of ten thoufand! I was this moment defying love and all his mifchief, and you are fent in the nick by him, to try my courage; but I'm above temptation, or below it—I duck down, and all his arrows fly over me.

D 2   A I R.

A I R.

Care flies from the lad that is merry,
　Who's heart is as found,
　And cheeks are as round,
As round, and as red as a cherry.

FIRST SHEPHERDESS.

What, are you always thus?

L I N C O.

Ay, or Heav'n help me! What would you have me do as you do—walking with your arms acrofs, thus—heighho'ing by the brook fide among the willows. Oh! fye for fhame, laffes! young and handfome, and fighing after one fellow a-piece, when you fhould have a hundred in a drove, following you like---like—you fhall have the fimile another time.

SECOND SHEPHERDESS.

No; prithee, Linco, give it us now.

L I N C O.

You fhall have it—or, what's better, I'll tell you what you are *not* like——you are not like our Shepherdefs Sylvia—fhe's fo cold, and fo coy, that fhe flies from her lovers, but is never without a fcore of them; you are always running after the fellows, and yet are always alone; a very great difference, let me tell you— froft and fire, that's all.

SECOND SHEPHERDESS.

Don't imagine, that I am in the pining condition my poor fifter is—I am as happy as fhe is miferable.

LINCO

L I N C O.
Good lack, I'm forry for't.

SECOND SHEPHERDESS.
What, forry that I am happy?

L I N C O.
O! no, prodigious glad.

FIRST SHEPHERDESS.
That I am miferable?

L I N C O.
No, no:—prodigious forry for that----and prodigious glad of the other.

FIRST SHEPHERDESS.
Be my friend, Linco; and I'll confefs my folly to you.——

L I N C O
Don't trouble yourfelf---'tis plain enough to be feen—but I'll give you a receipt for it without fee or reward—there's friendfhip for you.

FIRST SHEPERDESS.
Prithee, be ferious a little.

L I N C O.
No; Heav'n forbid! if I am ferious, 'tis all over with me—I fhould foon change my rofes for your lilies.

SECOND SHEPHERDESS.
Don't be impudent, Linco—But give us your receipt.

L I N C O.

A I R.

I laugh, and I fing,
I am blithfom and free,
The rogue's little fting,
It can never reach me:
*   For with fal, la, la, la!*
And ha, ha, ha, ha!
It can never reach me.

II.

My skin is so tough,
Or so blinking is he,
He can't pierce my buff,
Or he misses poor me.
    For with fal, la, la la!
    And ha, ha, ha, ha!
    He misses poor me.

III.

O, never be dull,
By the sad willow tree:
Of mirth be brim full,
And run over like me.
    For with fal, la, la, la!
    And ha, ha, ha, ha!
    Run over like me.

FIRST SHEPHERDESS.

It won't do!

LINCO.

Then you are far gone, indeed.

FIRST SHEPHERDESS.

And as I can't cure my love, I'll revenge it·

LINCO.

But how, how, shepherdess?

FIRST SHEPHERDESS.

I'll tear Sylvia's eyes out.

LINCO.

That's your only way—for you'll give your
nails a feast, and prevent mischief for the future
—Oh! tear her eyes out by all means.

SECOND

SECOND SHEPHERDESS.

How can you laugh, Linco, at my sister in her condition?

LINCO.

I must laugh at something; shall I be merry with you?

SECOND SHEPHERDESS.

The happy shepherd can bear to be laugh'd at.

LINCO.

Then Sylvia might take your shepherd without a sigh, tho' your sister would tear her eyes out.

SECOND SHEPHERDESS.

My shepherd! what does the fool mean?

FIRST SHEPHERDESS.

Her shepherd! pray tell us, Linco. (*Eagerly.*

LINCO.

'Tis no secret I suppose—I only met Damon and Sylvia together.

SECOND SHEPHERDESS.

What, *my* Damon?

LINCO.

Your Damon that was, and that would be Sylvia's Damon if she would accept of him.

SECOND SHEPHERDESS.

Her Damon! I'll make her to know----a wicked slut !-- a vile fellow—Come, sister, I'm ready to go with you—we'll give her her own— if our old governor continues to cast a sheep's eye at me, I'll have her turn'd out of Arcadia, I warrant you.

FIRST SHEPHERDESS.

This is some comfort, however, ha, ha, ha!

SECOND SHEPHERDESS.

Very well, sister! you may laugh, if you please—but perhaps it is too soon—Linco may be mistaken; it may be your Dorilas that was with her.

LINCO.

And your Damon too, and Strephon, and Colin, and Alexis, and Egon, and Croydon, and every fool of the parish but Linco, and he,

Sticks to fal, lal, la, la!
And ha, ha, ha!

FIRST SHEPHERDESS.

I can't bear to see him so merry, when I am so miserable.   [*Exit.*

SECOND SHEPHERDESS.

There is some satisfaction in seeing one's sister as miserable as one's self.   [*Exit.*

LINCO

Ha, ha, ha! O how the pretty sweet temper'd creatures are ruffled.

A I R.

This love puts 'em all in commotion,
For preach what you will,
They cannot be still,
No more than the wind or the ocean.   [*Exit.*

SCENE

S C E N E, *changes to a rural profpect.*

Sylvia *is difcover'd, lying upon a bank.*

Enter Merlin.

M E R L I N.

My art fucceeds—which hither has convey'd,
To catch the eye of Cymon, this fweet maid.
Her charms fhall clear the mifts which cloud his
 mind,
And make him warm, and fenfible, and kind;
Her yet cold heart with paffion's fighs fhall
 move,
Melt as he melts, and give him Love for Love.
This magic touch fhall to thefe flow'rs impart
 [*Touches a bafket of flowers with his wand.*
A power when beauty gains, to fix the heart;
A power, the falfe enchantrefs fhall confound;
And Cymon's *cure fhall be* Urganda's *wound.*
       [Exit.

Enter Cymon *with his Bird.*

C Y M O N.

Away, prifoner, and make yourfelf merry.
(*Bird flies.*) Ay, ay, I knew how it would be
with you—much good may it do you, Bob.—
What a fweet place this is! Hills, and greens,
and rocks, and trees, and water, and fun, and
birds!—Dear me, 'tis juft as if I had never feen
it before!

 [*Whiftles about till he fees* Sylvia, *then ftops and
  finks his whiftling by degrees, with a look and
  attitude of foolifh aftonifhment.*

  E   O la!

O la!—what's here!——'Tis something
dropp'd from the Heavens sure, and yet 'tis like
a woman too!—Bless me! is it alive! (*Sighs.*) It
can't be dead, for its cheek is as red as a rose,
and it moves about the heart of it—I am afraid
of it, and yet can't leave it.——I begin to
feel something strange here. (*Lays his hand on
his heart and sighs.*) I don't know what's the matter with me.—I wish it would wake, that I might
see its eyes.—If it should look gentle, and smile
upon me, I should be glad to play with it—Ay,
ay, there's something now in my breast that they
told me of—It feels oddly to me—and yet I don't
dislike it.

A I R.

All amaze!
Wonder, Praise,
Here for ever could I gaze!
    Creep still near it,   (advancing.)
    Yet I fear it,   (retiring.)
I can neither stay nor go,
    Can't forsake it,   (advancing.)
    Dare not wake it,   (retiring.)
Shall I touch it?—no, no, no!   (advances
                          and retires.)

II.

Cymon, sure thou art possest,
Something's got into thy breast,
    Gently stealing,
    Strangely feeling,
And my heart is panting so,
    I'm sad and merry, sick and well,
    What it is I cannot tell,
Makes me thus—heigho! heigho.

This stanza omitted in the acting.

I am

I am glad I came abroad!—I have not been
fo pleas'd ever fince I can remember—but, perhaps, it may be angry with me—I can't help it,
if it is.—I had rather fee her angry with me than
Urganda fmile upon me—Stay, ftay—(*Sylvia
ftirs.*) La, what a pretty foot it has!

(Cymon retires.)

Sylvia *raifing herfelf from the bank.*

A I R.

> *Yet awhile, fweet Sleep, deceive me,*
>   *Fold me in thy downy arms,*
> *Let not care awake to grieve me,*
>   *Lull it with thy potent charms.*
>
> *I, a turtle, doom'd to ftray,*
>   *Quitting young the parent's neft,*
> *Find each bird a bird of prey;*
>   *Sorrow knows not where to reft.*

[Sylvia *fees* Cymon *with emotion, while he gazes
ftrongly on her, and retires gently, pulling off
his cap.*

S Y L V I A, (confufed)

Who's that?

C Y M O N.

'Tis I.   (*bowing and hefitating.*)

S Y L V I A.

What's your name?

C Y M O N.

Cymon.

S Y L V I A.

What do you want, young man?

E 2   CYMON.

C Y M O N.

Nothing, young woman.

S Y L V I A.

What are you doing there?

C Y M O N.

Looking at you there.

S Y L V I A.

What a pretty creature it is!   (*Afide.*)

C Y M O N.

What eyes it has!   (*Afide.*)

S Y L V I A.

You don't intend me any harm?

C Y M O N.

Not I indeed!—I wifh you don't do me fome.
Are you a fairy, pray?

S Y L V I A.

No—I am a poor harmlefs fhepherdefs.

C Y M O N.

I don't know that—You have bewitch'd me,
I believe.

S Y L V I A.

Indeed, I have not; and if it was in my power
to harm you, I'm fure it is not in my inclination.

C Y M O N.

I'm fure, I would truft you to do any thing
with me.

S Y L V I A.

Would you?   (*Sighs.*)

C Y M O N.

Yes, indeed, I would.   (*Sighs.*)

SYLVIA.

S Y L V I A.

Why do you look fo at me?

C Y M O N.

Why do you look fo at me?

S Y L V I A.

I can't help it. (*Sighs.*)

C Y M O N.

Nor I neither—(*Sighs.*) I wifh you'd fpeak to me, and look at me, as Urganda does.

S Y L V I A.

What the Enchantrefs? Do you belong to her?

C Y M O N.

I had rather belong to you—I would not defire to go abroad, if I did.

S Y L V I A.

Does Urganda love you?

C Y M O N.

So fhe fays.

S Y L V I A.

I'm forry for it.

C Y M O N.

Why are you forry, pray?

S Y L V I A.

I fhall never fee you again—I wifh I had not feen you now!

C Y M O N.

If you did but wifh as I do, all the enchantreffes in the world could not hinder us from feeing one another.

4　　　　　　　　　SYLVIA.

SYLVIA.

Do you love Urganda?

CYMON.

Do you love the Shepherds?

SYLVIA.

I did not know what Love was this morning.

CYMON.

Nor I, 'till this afternoon.—Who taught you, pray?

SYLVIA.

Who taught you?

CYMON.

(*Bashful.*) You.

SYLVIA.

(*Blushing.*) You.

CYMON.

You could teach me any thing, if I was to live with you—I should not be call'd Simple Cymon any more.

SYLVIA.

Nor I, hard-hearted Sylvia.

CYMON.

Sylvia—what a sweet name!—I could speak it for ever. (*Transported.*)

SYLVIA.

I can never forget that of Cymon: Tho' Cymon may forget me. (*sighs.*)

CYMON.

Never, never, my sweet Sylvia. [*Falls on his knees, and kisses her hand.*

SYLVIA.

S Y L V I A.

We fhall be feen and feparated for ever! Pray let me go—we are undone if we are feen——I muft go—I am all over in a flutter!

C Y M O N.

When fhall I fee you again?—In half an hour?

S Y L V I A.

Half an hour! that will be too foon——No, no, it muft be—three quarters of an hour.

C Y M O N.

And where, my fweet Sylvia?

S Y L V I A.

Any where, my fweet Cymon.

C Y M O N.

In the grove by the river there.

S Y L V I A.

And you fhall take this to remember it. (*Gives him the nofegay enchanted by* Merlin.) I wifh it were a kingdom, I would give it you, and a queen along with it.

C Y M O N.

How my heart is tranfported!——and here is one for you too; which is of no value to me, unlefs you will receive it—take it, my fweet *Sylvia.* [Cymon *gives her* Urganda's *nofegay.*

D U E T.

D U E T.

Syl. *O take this nosegay, gentle youth,*
Cym. *And you, sweet maid, take mine;*
Syl. *Unlike these flowers, be thy fair truth;*
Cym. *Unlike these flowers be thine.*
   These changing soon,
    Will soon decay,
   Be sweet till noon,
    Then pass away.
Fair for a time their transient charms appear;
But truth unchang'd shall bloom for ever here.
    [Each preffing their Hearts.
      [*Exeunt.*

END *of the* SECOND ACT.

A C T III.

SCENE, *before* Urganda's *Palace.*

Enter Urganda *and* Fatima.

URGANDA.

IS he not return'd yet, Fatima?

FATIMA.

He has no feelings but thofe of hunger; when that pinches him, he'll return to be fed, like other animals.

URGANDA.

Indeed, Fatima, his infenfibility aftonifhes and diftracts me.—I have exhaufted all my arts to overcome it; I have run all dangers to make an impreffion upon him; and, inftead of finding my paffion in the leaft abated by his ingratitude, I am only a greater flave to my weaknefs, and more incapable of relief.

FATIMA.

Why then I may as well hold my tongue—but before I would wafte all the prime of my womanhood in playing fuch a lofing game, I would—but I fee you don't mind me, madam, and therefore I'll fay no more—I know the confequence, and muft fubmit.

F

U R G A N D A.

What can I do in my fituation?

F A T I M A.

What you ought to do—and you belye your beauty and underftanding by not doing it.

U R G A N D A.

Explain yourfelf.

F A T I M A.

To fecure my tongue, and your honour, (for Merlin will have you by hook or by crook) marry him directly—it will prevent mifchief at leaft—fo much for prudence.—During your honey-moon, I will hide the young gentleman, and if he has any tinder in him, kindle him up for you. If your hufband fhould be tired of you, as ten to one he will, I'll ftep in his way, he may be glad of the change, and in return, I'll reftore young Simplicity to you.—That's what I call a fafhionable fcheme.

U R G A N D A.

I can't bear trifling at this time—you'll make me angry with you.—But fee where Cymon approaches—he feems tranfported—Look, look, Fatima! He is kiffing and embracing my nofegay—it has had the defired effect, and I am happy—we'll be invifible, that I may obferve his tranfports.

Urganda *waves her wand, and retires with* Fatima.

Enter Cymon, *hugging a nofegay.*

C Y M O N.

Oh my dear, fweet, charming nofegay!—To fee thee, to fmell thee, and to tafte thee, (*Kiffes*

　　　　　　　　　　　it.)

it.) will make Urganda and her garden delightful to me.   (*Kiſſes it.*)

FATIMA.

What does he ſay?

URGANDA.

Huſh, huſh!—all tranſport, and about me?
What a change is this?

C Y M O N.

With this I can want for nothing.—I poſſeſs
every thing with this.—My mind and heart are
expanded: I feel—I know not what.—Every
thought that delights, and every paſſion that
tranſports, gather, like ſo many bees, about
this treaſure of ſweetneſs.—Oh, the dear, dear
noſegay, and the dear, dear giver of it!

URGANDA.

The dear, dear giver. —Mind that, Fatima!
What heavenly eloquence! Here's a change of
heart and mind!—heigho!—

FATIMA.

I'm all amazement!—in a dream!—but is that
your noſegay?

URGANDA.

Mine! how can you doubt it?

FATIMA.

Nay, I'm near ſighted.

C Y M O N.

She has not a beauty that is not brought to
mind by theſe flowers.—This is the colour of her
hair—this of her ſkin—this of her cheeks—this
of her eyes—this of her lips—ſweet, ſweet—
and thoſe roſe buds—Oh! I ſhall go out of my
wits with pleaſure!

F 2   FATIMA.

F A T I M A.

'Tis pity to lose 'em the moment you have found 'em.——

U R G A N D A.

O Fatima! I never was proud of my power, or vain of my beauty, till this transporting moment!

C Y M O N.

Where shall I put it? Where shall I conceal it from every body?—I'll keep it in my bosom, next my heart, all the day; and at night, I will put it upon my pillow, and talk to it—and sigh to it—and swear to it—and sleep by it—and kiss it for ever and ever!

A I R.

What exquisite pleasure!
This sweet treasure
From me they shall never
    Sever;
In thee, in thee,
My charmer I see.
I'll sigh, and caress thee,
I'll kiss thee, and press thee
Thus, thus, to my bosom for ever and ever.

Urganda *and* Fatima *come forward,*
Cymon *starts at seeing* Urganda, *and puts the nosegay in his bosom with great confusion.*

U R G A N D A.   (*Smiling.*)

Pray, what is that you would kiss, and press to your bosom for ever and ever?

C Y M O N.

Nothing but the end of an old song the shepherds taught me, " *I'll sigh and caress thee, I'll*
                           kiss

kifs thee and prefs thee,"—that's all—

[*Pretends to fing.*

F A T I M A.

Upon my word! a very hopeful youth indeed, and much improved in his finging—What think you know ?   [*Afide to* Urganda.

U R G A N D A.

Nothing but his bafhfulnefs ftruggling with his paffion. What was that you was talking to ?

C Y M O N.

Myfelf, to be fure, I had nothing elfe to talk to.

U R G A N D A.

Yes, but you have, Cymon—don't be afham'd of what you ought to be proud of—there is fomething in your bofom, next you heart.

C Y M O N.

Yes, fo there is.

U R G A N D A.

What is it, Cymon ?   (*Smiling.*)

F A T I M A.

Now his modefty is giving way ; we fhall have him at laft.   (*afide.*

C Y M O N.

Nothing but a nofegay.

U R G A N D A.

That which I gave you ?—let me fee it.

C Y M O N.

What! give a thing, and take it away again ?

U R G A N D A.

I would not take it away for the world.

CYMON.

C Y M O N.

Nor would I give it you, for a hundred worlds.

F A T I M A.

See it by all means, madam.----I have my reasons. *(aside to* Urganda.)

U R G A N D A.

I muſt ſee it, Cymon, and therefore no delay ---you cannot have the love you ſeem'd to have but now, and refuſe me.

C Y M O N.

O but I can, and for that reaſon.

U R G A N D A.

Don't provoke me—I will ſee it, or ſhut you up for ever.

C Y M O N.

What a ſtir is here about nothing! Now are you ſatisfied?

[*He holds the noſegay at a diſtance.* Urganda *and* Fatima *look at one another with ſurprize.*

F A T I M A.

I was right.

U R G A N D A.

And I am miſerable!

C Y M O N.

Have you ſeen it enough?

U R G A N D A.

That is not mine, Cymon.

C Y M O N.

No—'tis mine.

U R G A N D A.

Who gave it you?

C Y M O N.

A perfon.

U R G A N D A.

What perfon—male or female?

C Y M O N.

La! how can I tell?

F A T I M A.

Finely improved indeed!—a genius! (*afide.*)

U R G A N D A.

I muft diffemble. (*afide.*) Lookee, Cymon;
I did but fport with you—the nofegay was your
own, and you had a right to give it away, or
throw it away.

C Y M O N.

Indeed, but I did not—I only gave it for this
—which as it is fo much finer and fweeter, I
thought would not vex you.

U R G A N D A.

Heigho! (*afide.*)

F A T I M A.

Vex her! O not in the leaft.—But you fhould
not have given away her prefent to a vulgar
creature.

C Y M O N.

How dare you talk to me fo? I would have
you to know, fhe is neither ugly, nor vulgar.

F A T I M A.

Oh fhe!—your humble fervant, young Simplicity!---La, how can you tell whether it is
male or female!

(*Mimicks* Cymon, *who feems confounded.*

URGANDA.

Don't mind her impertinence, Cymon—I give you leave to follow your own inclinations.—I brought you hither for your pleasure, indulge yourself in every thing you like—and be as happy as following your desires can make you.

CYMON.

Then I am happy, indeed—thank you, Lady, you have made me quite another creature! I'm out of my wits with joy—I may follow my inclinations—thank you, and thank you, and thank you again.

" I'll sigh and caress thee,
" I'll kiss thee, and press thee
" Thus, thus, to my bosom for ever and
" ever."— [*Exit* Cymon *singing.*

FATIMA.

You are a philosopher, indeed!

URGANDA.

A female one—Fatima: I have hid the most racking jealousy under this false appearance, in order to deceive him.— I shall by this means discover the cause of his joy, and my misery; and when that is known, you shall see whether I am most of a woman, or a philosopher.

FATIMA.

Ill lay ten to one of the woman, in matters of this nature.

URGANDA.

Let him have liberty to go wherever he pleases—I will have him watch'd; that office be your's, my faithful Fatima—about it instantly—don't lose sight of him—no reply—not a word more.——

F A T I M A.

That's very hard—but I'm gone. [*Exit*.

U R G A N D A.

When I have difcover'd the object of his prefent tranfports, I will make her more wretched
than any of her fex——except myfelf.

A I R.

Hence every hope, and every fear !
  Awake, awake, my power and pride,
Let Jealoufy, ftern Jealoufy appear !
  With Vengeance at her fide !

II.

Who fcorns my charms, my power fhall prove.
  Revenge fucceeds to flighted love !
  Revenge !—But Oh, my fighing heart
    With rebel Love takes part ;
    Now pants again with all her fears,
    And drowns her rage in tears. [Exit.

SCENE, Dorcas's Cottage.

Sylvia *at the door with* Cymon's *nofegay in her hand.*

A I R.

Thefe flowers, like our hearts, are united in one,
And are bound up fo foft, that they can't be undone ;
So well are they blended, fo beauteous to fight,
There fprings from their union a tenfold delight ;
Nor poifon, nor weed here, our paffion to warn ;
But fweet without briar, the rofe without thorn.

G   The

The more I look upon this nosegay, the more I feel Cymon in my heart and mind——Ever since I have seen him, heard his vows, and received this nosegay from him, I am in continual agitation, and cannot rest a moment.—— I wander without knowing where——I speak without knowing to whom,——and I look without knowing at what.——Heigho! how my poor heart flutters in my breast!——Now I dread to lose him,——and now again I think him mine for ever!

A I R.

O why should we sorrow, who never knew sin!
Let smiles of content shew our rapture within :
This love has so rais'd me, I now tread in air !
He's sure sent from Heav'n to lighten my care!

II.

Each shepherdess views me with scorn and disdain !
Each shepherd pursues me, but all is in vain :
No more will I sorrow, no longer despair,
He's sure sent from Heav'n to lighten my care !

(LINCO *is seen listening to her singing.*)

L I N C O.

If you were as wicked, shepherdess, as you are innocent, that voice of your's would corrupt justice herself, unless she was deaf, as well as blind.

S Y L V I A.

I hope you did not overhear me, Linco?

L I N C O.

O, but I did tho'—and, notwithſtanding I come as the deputy of a deputy governor, to bring you before my principal, for ſome complaints made againſt you by a certain ſhepherdeſs, I will ſtand your friend, tho' I loſe my place for it——there are not many ſuch friends, ſhepherdeſs.

S Y L V I A.

What have I done to the ſhepherdeſſes, that they perſecute me ſo?

L I N C O.

You are much too handſome, which is a crime the beſt of 'em can't forgive you.

S Y L V I A.

I'll truſt myſelf with you, and face my ene-mies.

[*As they are going*, Dorcas *calls from the Cottage.*

D O R C A S.

Where are you going, child?—Who is that with you, Sylvia?

L I N C O.

Now ſhall we be ſtopp'd by this good old wo-man, who will know all—and can ſcarce hear any thing.

D O R C A S (*coming forward.*)

I'll ſee who you have with you.

L I N C O.

'Tis I, dame, your kinſman Linco.
                    (*Speaks loud in her ear.*

DORCAS.

D O R C A S.

O, is it you, honeſt Linco! (*Takes his hand.*)
Well, what's to do now.

L I N C O,

The governor deſires to ſpeak with Sylvia;
a friendly enquiry, that's all.   (*Speaks loud.*)

D O R C A S.

For what, for what—tell me that—I have
nothing to do with his deſires, nor ſhe neither
——he is grown very inquiſitive of late about
ſhepherdeſſes —Fine doings, indeed! No ſuch
doings when I was young—if he wants to examine any body, why don't he examine me? I'll
give him an anſwer, let him be as inquiſitive
as he pleaſes.

L I N C O,

But I am your kinſman, dame, and you dare
truſt me ſure.   (*Speaks loud.*

D O R C A S.

Thou art the beſt of 'em, that I'll ſay for thee
—but the beſt of you are bad when a young
woman is in the caſe—I have gone through great
difficulties myſelf, I can aſſure you, in better
times than theſe: why muſt not I go too?

L I N C O.

We ſhall return to you again—before you can
get there.   (*Still ſpeaking loud.*)

S Y L V I A.

You may truſt us, mother,—my own innocence, and Linco's goodneſs, will be guard
enough for me.

DORCAS.

Eh! what!

LINCO.

She fays, you may truſt me with her innocence.   (*Speaking louder.*

DORCAS.

Well, well—I will then—thou art a ſweet
creature, and I love thee better than even I did
my own child—(*kiſſes* Sylvia.) When thou art
fetched away by him that brought thee, 'twill
be a woeful day for me.—Well, well, go thy
ways with Linco—I dare truſt thee any where
—I'll prepare thy dinner at thy return; and bring
my honeſt kinſman along with you.

LINCO.

We will be with you, before you can make
the pot boil.

DORCAS.

Before what!

LINCO.

We will be with you, before you can make
the pot boil.
(*Speaks very loud, and goes off with* Sylvia.

DORCAS.

Heav'n ſhield thee, for the ſweeteſt, beſt
creature that ever bleſt old age—What a comfort
ſhe is to me! All I have to wiſh for in this world,
is to know who thou art, who brought thee to
me, and then to ſee thee as happy as thou haſt
made poor Dorcas. What can the governor want
with her?—I wiſh I had gone too—I'd have
talk'd to him, and to the purpoſe—We had
no ſuch doings when I was a young woman!
they never made ſuch a fuſs with me!

AIR.

A I R.

When I were young, tho' now am old,
The men were kind and true;
But now they're grown so false and bold, ·
What can a woman do?
Now what can a woman do?
For men are truly,
So unruly,
I tremble at seventy-two!

II.

When I were fair—tho' now so so,
No hearts were given to rove,
Our pulses beat nor fast, nor slow,
But all was faith and love;
What can a woman do?
Now what can a woman do?
For men are truly,
So unruly,
I tremble at seventy-two!   [Exit.

S C E N E, *the Magistrate's House.*

Enter Dorus, *and Second Shepherdess.*

D O R U S.

This way, this way, damsel——now we are alone, I can hear your grievances, and will redress them, that I will——you have my good liking, damsel, and favour follows of course.

SECOND SHEPHERDESS.

I want words, your honour and worship, to thank you fitly.

DORUS.

D O R U S.

Smile upon me, damfel——Smile, and command me——your hand is whiter than ever, I proteft——you muft indulge me with a chafte falute.   (*kiffes her hand.*

S E C O N D   S H E P H E R D E S S.

La! your honour. (*Curtfies.*)

D O R U S.

You have charm'd me, damfel; and I can deny you nothing—another chafte falute—'tis a perfect cordial—(*kiffes her hand.*) Well, what. fhall I do with this Sylvia, this ftranger, this baggage, that has affronted thee? I'll fend her where fhe fhall never vex thee again—an impudent, wicked—(*kiffes her hand.*) I'll fend her packing this very day.

S E C O N D   S H E H E P R D E S S.

I vow your worfhip is too good to me.
                                (*Leering at him.*

D O R U S.

Nothing's too good for thee——I'll fend her off directly.—Don't fret and teaze thyfelf about her——go fhe fhall, and fpeedily too.——I have fent my deputy Linco for that Dorcas, who has harbour'd this Sylvia without my knowledge, and the country fhall be rid of her to-morrow morning.——Smile upon me, damfel—fmile upon me.

S E C O N D   S H E P H E R D E S S.

I wou'd I were half as handfome as Sylvia, I might fmile to good purpofe.

D O R U S.

I'll Sylvia her! an impudent vagrant——She can neither fmile or whine to any purpofe, while I am to govern.—She fhall go to-morrow, damfel——this hand, this lily hand, has fign'd her fate.　(*kiffes it.*)

Enter Linco.

L I N C O.

No bribery and corruption, I beg of your honour.

D O R U S.

You are too bold, Linco——Where did you learn this impertinence to your fuperiors?

L I N C O.

From an old fong, and pleafe your honour, where I get all my wifdom——Heav'n help me.

A I R.

If fhe whifpers the judge, be he ever fo wife,
　Tho' great and important his truft is;
His hand is unfteady, a pair of black eyes
　Will kick up the balance of juftice.

II.

If his paffions are ftrong, his judgment grows weak,
　For love thro' his veins will be creeping;
And his worfhip, when near to a round dimple cheek,
　Tho' he ought to be blind, will be peeping.

DORUS.

DORUS.

Poo, poo, 'tis a very foolifh fong, and you're a fool for finging it.

SECOND SHEPHERDESS.

Linco's no friend of mine; Sylvia can fing, and has enchanted him.

LINCO.

My ears have been feafted, that's moft certain —but my heart, damfel, is as uncrack'd as your virtue, or his honour's wifdom. There is not too much prefumption in that, I hope.

DORUS.

Linco, do your duty, and know your diftance —What is come to the fellow? he is fo altered, I don't know him again.

LINCO.

Your honour's eye-fight is not fo good as it was—I am always the fame, and Heav'n forbid that mirth fhould be a fin—I am always laughing and finging —let who will change, I will not.— I laugh at the times, but I can't mend 'em—They are woefully alter'd for the worfe— but here's my comfort.

[Shewing his tabor and pipe.

DORUS.

I'll hear no more of this ribaldry—I hate poetry, and I don't like mufick—Where is this vagrant, this Sylvia?

LINCO.

In the juftice-chamber, waiting for your honour's commands.

DORUS.

Why did not you tell me fo?

H

L I N C O

I thought your honour better engaged, and that it was too much for you to try two female caufes at one time.

D O R U S.

You thought! I won't have you think, but obey—Times are chang'd indeed! Deputies muft not think for their fuperiors.

L I N C O.

Muft not, they! What will become of our poor country!   (*going.*

D O R U S.

No more, impertinence, but bring the culprit hither.

L I N C O.

In the twinkling of your honour's eye. [*Exit.*

S E C O N D   S H E P H E R D E S S.

I leave my griefs in your worfhip's hands.

D O R U S.

You leave 'em in my heart, damfel, where they foon fhall be changed into pleafures—wait for me in the juftice chamber—Smile, damfel, fmile upon me, and edge the fword of juftice.

Enter Linco *and* Sylvia.

S E C O N D   S H E P H E R D E S S.

Here fhe comes; fee how like an innocent fhe looks—But I'll be gone—I truft in your worfhip—I hate the fight of her—I cou'd tear her nafty eyes out.   [*Exit*

DORUS.

D O R U S.

[Gazing at Sylvia.
Hem, hem! I am told, young woman—hem, hem!—that—she does not look so mischievous as I expected. *[Aside, and turning from her.*

L I N C O.

Bear up, sweet shepherdess! your beauty and innocence will put injustice out of countenance.

S Y L V I A.

The shame of being suspected confounds me, and I can't speak.

D O R U S.

Where is the old woman, Dorcas, they told me of? Did not I order you to bring her before me?

L I N C O.

The good old woman is so deaf, and your reverence a little thick of hearing, I thought the business would be sooner and better done by the young woman.

D O R U S.

What at your thinking again--Young shepherdess, I hear—I hear—Hem!—Her modesty pleases me.(*Aside.*)—What is the reason, I say—Hem!—that—that I hear—She has very fine features.
[Aside, and turning from her.

L I N C O.

Speak, speak, Sylvia, and the business is done.

D O R U S.

Is not your name Sylvia?

H 2

L I N C O.

Yes, your honour, her name is Sylvia.

D O R U S.

I don't afk you — What is your name? look
up and tell me, fhepherdefs.

S Y L V I A.

Sylvia.!   *(Sighs and curtfies.*

D O R U S.

What a fweet look with her eyes fhe has!
(*Afide.*)   What can be the reafon, Sylvia —that
that—Hem! I proteft fhe difarms my anger.
              [*Afide, and turns from her.*

L I N C O.

Now is your time; fpeak to his reverence.

D O R U S.

Don't whifper the prifoner.

S Y L V I A.

Prifoner! Am I a prifoner then?

D O R U S.

No, not abfolutely a prifoner; but you are
charged, damfel—Hem, hem—charged, damfel
—I don't know what to fay to her.
              [*Afide and turns from her.*

S Y L V I A.

With what, your honour?

L I N C O.

If he begins to damfel us, we have him
fure,

              2   SYLVIA,

S Y L V I A.

What is my crime?

L I N C O.

A little too handsome, that's all.

D O R U S.

Hold your peace—Why don't you look up in my face if you are innocent? (Sylvia *looks at* Dorus *with great modesty.*) I can't stand it— she has turn'd my anger, my justice, and my whole scheme, topsy-turvy—Reach me a chair, Linco.

L I N C O.

One sweet song, Sylvia, before his reverence gives sentence.   [*Reaches a chair for* Dorus.

D O R U S.

No singing, her looks have done too much already.

L I N C O.

Only to soften your rigour.

Sylvia *sings.*

A I R.

From duty if the shepherd stray,
  And leave his flocks to feed,
The wolf will seize the harmless prey,
  And innocence will bleed.

II.

In me a harmless lamb behold,
  Opprest with every fear ;
O guard, good shepherd, guard your fold,
  For wicked wolves are near.

[*Kneels.*

DORUS.

D O R U S.

I'll guard thee, and fold thee too, my lambkin
—and they shan't hurt thee—This is a melting
ditty indeed! Rise, rise, my Sylvia.

[*Embraces her.*

Enter Second Shepherdess.

[Dorus *and she start at seeing each other.*

S E C O N D   S H E P H E R D E S S.

Is your reverence taking leave of her before
you drive her out of the country?

D O R U S.

How now! What presumption is this, to
break in upon us so, and interrupt the course of
justice?

S E C O N D   S H E P H E R D E S S.

May I be permitted to speak three words with
your worship?—

D O R U S.

Well, well, I will speak to you—I'll come to
you in the the justice-chamber presently.

S E C O N D   S H E P H E R D E S S.

I knew the wheedling slut would spoil all—but
I'll be up with her yet.   [*Aside and Ex.*

D O R U S.

I'm glad she's gone—Linco, you must send
her away—I won't see her now.

L I N C O.

And shall I take Sylvia to prison?

D O R U S.

No, no, no; to prison! mercy forbid! —
What a sin should I have committed to
                                        please

pleafe that envious, jealous-pated fhepherdefs?—
Linco, comfort the damfel—Dry your eyes,
Sylvia—I will call upon you myfelf—and examine
Dorcas myfelf—and protect you myfelf—and do
every thing myfelf—I profefs fhe has bewitched
me—I am all agitation—I'll call upon you to-
morrow—perhaps to-night—perhaps in half an
hour--Take care of her, Linco--fhe has bewitched
me, and I fhall lofe my wits if I look on her any
longer—Oh! the fweet, lovely, pretty, delightful
creature!

L I N C O.

Don't whimper now, my fweet Sylvia—
Juftice has taken up the fword and fcales again,
and your rivals fhall cry their eyes out—The
day's our own.

A I R.

> Sing high derry derry,
>   The day is our own,
> Be wife and be merry,
>   Let forrow alone ;
>   Alter your tone,
> To high derry derry,
>   Be wife and be merry.
>   The day is our own.

[*Exeunt.*

END *of the* THIRD ACT.

A C T IV.

SCENE, *an old Castle.*

Enter URGANDA, *greatly agitated.*

U R G A N D A.

LOST, lost Urganda!—Nothing can controul
 The beating tempest of my restless soul!
While I prepare, in this dark witching hour,
My potent spells, and call forth all my power—
Arise, ye demons of revenge, arise!
Begin your rites—unseen by mortal eyes;
Hurl plagues and mischiefs thro' the poison'd air,
And give me vengeance to appease despair!

Chorus—(*underground*) We come, we come, we
 come. (*She waves her wand, and the castle
 vanishes.*)

  The first Demon of revenge arises.

A I R.

While mortals charm their cares in sleep,
 And demons howl below,
Urganda *calls us from the deep;*
 Arise, ye sons of woe!
  Ever busy, ever willing,
  All those horrid tasks fulfilling,
 Which draw from mortal breasts the groan,
 And make their torments like our own.

Chorus—(*underground*) We come, we come, we
   come!

Demons

Demons arife and perform their rites.

Then Exeunt, *with* Urganda *at their head.*

S C E N E, *the Country.*

Enter Linco, *drawing in* Damon *and* Dorilas.

L I N C O

Nay, nay, but let me talk to you a little—by
the lark you are early ftirrers—has not that gad-
fly jealoufy ftung you up to this fame mifchief
you are upon ?

D A M O N.

We are commanded by our governor, who
has orders from Urganda to bring Cymon and
Sylvia before her.

L I N C O,

And you are fond of this employment, are you?
fye, for fhame—I know more than you think I
know.—You were each of you (good fouls!) be-
troth'd to two fhepherdeffes—but Sylvia comes
in the nick, and away 'go vows, promifes, and
proteftations—fhe loving Cymon, and defpifing
you—and you.—You (hating one another) join
cordially to diftrefs them for loving one another
—fye, for fhame, fhepherds !

D A M O N.

What will the governor fay to this? This is
fine treatment of your betters.

L I N C O.

If my betters are no better than they fhould
be, 'tis their fault, and not mine—Urganda,
Dorus, and you, not being able to reach the

I   grapes,

grapes, won't let any body elfe tafte them—fye, for fhame, fhepherds!

D A M O N.

We have no time to lofe—we muft raife the fhepherds, and hunt after thefe young finners; and you, Mr. Deputy, for all your airs, muft make one in the chafe.

L I N C O.

Before I would follow unlawful game to pleafe a hot-liver'd enchantrefs, an old itching governor, and two fuch jealous-pated noodles as yourfelves, I would thruft my pipe through my tabor, chuck it into the river, and myfelf after it.

D A M O N.

Here comes the governor; now we fhall hear what you will fay to him.

L I N C O.

Juft what I have faid to you; an honeft laughing fellow, like myfelf, don't mind a governor, though I fhould raife his fpleen, and lofe my place into the bargain—there are not many deputies in Arcadia of the fame mind.

D O R I L A S.

Come, come, let us mind our bufinefs, and not his impertinence.

D A M O N.

If the governor would do as I wifh him, you would have your deferts, Mr. Deputy Linco.

L I N C O.

And if Cymon could do as I wifh him, you would have your deferts, my gentle fhepherds.

Enter

Enter Dorus *and* Arcadians.

D O R U S.

Where have you been, Linco? I fent for you an hour ago.

L I N C O.

I was in bed, your honour; and as I don't walk in my fleep, I could not be well with you before I was drefs'd.

D O R U S.

No joking—no joking—we are ordered by the Enchantrefs to fearch for Cymon and Sylvia, and bring them before her.

L I N C O.

I hate to fpoil fport — fo I'll go home again.
                                    (*Going.*)

D O R U S.

Stay, Linco (*he returns*). I command you to do your duty, and go with me in purfuit of thefe young criminals.

L I N C O.

Criminals! heaven blefs them, I fay!—I'll go home again.   (*Going.*)

D O R U S.

Was there ever fuch infolence! Come back, Linco; how dare you difobey what I order, and Urganda commands? Give me an anfwer.

L I N C O.

Confcience! confcience! Governor—an old fafhion'd excufe, but a true one——I cannot find in my heart to difturb two fweet young creatures—whom as heaven has put together, I will not attempt to divide;—'twould be a crying fin!—I'll go home again.   (*Going.*

D O R U S.

You are a fcandal to your place, and you fhall hold it no longer; I'll take it from you inftantly.

L I N C O.

You cannot take from me a quiet confcience and a merry heart;---you are heartily welcome to all the reft, Governor.

D O R U S.

I difmifs you from this moment---you fhall be no deputy of mine—you fhall fuffer for your arrogance;---I fhall tell the Enchantrefs that you are leagu'd with this Sylvia, and will not do your duty.

L I N C O.

A word with your honour---could you have been leagu'd with this Sylvia too, you would not have done your duty, Mr. Governor.

D O R U S.

Hem !---Come along, fhepherds, and don't mind his impudence.

[*Exeunt* Dorus *and Shepherds.*

L I N C O.

I wifh your reverence a good morning, and I thank you for all favours—any fool now that was lefs merry than myfelf, would be out of fpirits for being out of place;—but as matters are now turn'd topfy turvy, I won't walk upon my head for the beft office in Arcadia---And fo my

virtuous

virtuous old governor, get what deputy you
pleaſe; I ſhall ſtick to my tabor and pipe, and
ſing away the loſs of one place, till I can whiſtle
myſelf into another.

A I R.

When peace here was reigning,
And love without waining,
Or care or complaining,
Baſe paſſions diſdaining;
 This, this was my way,
  With my pipe and my tabor,
 I laugh'd down the day,
  Nor envy'd the joys of my neighbour.

II.

Now ſad transformation
Runs thro' the whole nation;
Peace, love, recreation,
All chang'd to vexation;
 This, this is my way,
  With my pipe and my tabor,
 I laugh down the day,
  And pity the cares of my neighbour.

III.

While all are deſigning,
Their friends undermining,
Reviling, repining,
To miſchief inclining;
 This, this is my way,
  With my pipe and my tabor,
 I laugh down the day,
  And pity the cares of my neighbour.

Omitted in the repreſentation.

        [Exit.

S C E N E,

SCENE, *another Part of the Country.*

Enter FATIMA.

Truly a very pretty mifchievous errand I am
fent upon—I am to follow this foolifh young
fellow all about to find out his haunts—not fo
foolifh neither, for he is fo much improved of
late, we fhrewdly fufpect that he muft have fome
female to fharpen his intellects—For love, among
many other ftrange things, can make fools of
wits, and wits of fools. I faw our young par-
tridge run before me, and take cover here-
abouts; I muft make no noife, for fear of alarm-
ing him; befides, I hate to difturb the poor
things in pairing time.

[*Looks thro' the bufhes.*

Enter MERLIN.

MERLIN.

I fhall fpoil your peeping, thou evil counfellor
of a faithlefs miftrefs—I muft torment her a little
for her good—Such females muft feel much to
be made juft and reafonable creatures.

Fatima, *peeping thro' the bufhes.*

There they are—our fool has made no bad
choice—Upon my word, a very pretty couple!
and will make my poor lady's heart ach.

MERLIN.

I fhall twinge yours a little before we part.

FATIMA.

Well faid, Cymon! upon your knees to her!
Now for my pocket-book, that I may exactly
defcribe

defcribe this rival of ours ; fhe is much too handfome to live long, fhe will be either burnt alive,
thrown to wild beafts, or fhut up in the Black
Tower—the greateft mercy fhe can have will be
to let her take her choice.

[Takes out a pocket-book.

M E R L I N.

May be fo—but we will prevent the prophecy,
if we can.

Fatima, *writing in her book.*

She is of a good height, about my fize—a
fine fhape, delicate features—charming hair—
heav'nly eyes; not unlike my own—with fuch a
fweet fmile ! She muft be burnt alive ! yes, yes,
fhe muft be burnt alive.

[Merlin *taps her upon the fhoulder with his wand.*

F A T I M A.

Who's there! blefs me !—Nobody—I proteft
it ftartled me. I muft finifh my picture.

[Writes on.
[Merlin *waves his wand over her head.*

Now let me fee what I have written.—Blefs
me, what's here! all the letters are as red as
blood—My eyes fail me! Sure I am bewitched
(*Reads and trembles.*) Urganda *has a fhameful paf-
fion for* Cymon, Cymon *a moft virtuous one for*
Sylvia ;—*as for* Fatima, *wild beafts, the Black
Tower, and burning alive, are too good for her.*
(*Drops the book.*) I have not power to ftir a ftep
—I knew what would come of affronting that
devil Merlin. [Merlin *is vifible.*

M E R L I N.

True, Fatima, and I am here at your fervice.

FATIMA.

O moſt magnanimous Merlin! don't ſet your wit to a poor fooliſh weak woman.

MERLIN.

Why, then, will a fooliſh weak woman ſet her wit to me? But we will be better friends for the future—Mark me, Fatima. [*Holds up his wand.*

FATIMA.

No conjuration, I beſeech your worſhip, and you ſhall do any thing with me.

MERLIN.

I want nothing of you but to hold your tongue.

FATIMA.

Will nothing elſe content your fury?

MERLIN.

Silence, babler.

FATIMA.

I am your own for ever, moſt merciful Mer-lin! I am your own for ever—O my poor tongue! I thought I never ſhould have wagg'd thee again—What a dreadful thing it would be to be dumb?

MERLIN.

You ſee it is not in the power of Urganda to protect you, or to injure Cymon and Sylvia—I will be their protector againſt all her arts, tho' ſhe has leagu'd herſelf with the demons of re-venge—We have no power but what reſults from our virtue.

FATIMA.

I had rather loſe any thing than my ſpeech.

MERLIN.

M E R L I N.

As you profeſs yourſelf my friend (for, with
all my art, I cannot ſee into a woman's mind) I
will ſhew my gratitude, and my power, by giving your tongue an additional accompliſhment.

F A T I M A.

What, ſhall I talk more than ever ?

M E R L I N.   *(Smiling.)*

That would be no accompliſhment, Fatima.
—No, I mean that you ſhould talk leſs—When
you return to Urganda, ſhe will be very inquiſitive, and you very ready to tell her all you
know.

F A T I M A.

And may I without offence to your worſhip ?

M E R L I N.

Silence, and mark me well—obſerve me truly
and punctually. Every anſwer you give to Urganda's queſtions, muſt be confined to two words,
Yes and *No*—I have done you a great favour,
and you don't perceive it.

F A T I M A.

Not very clearly, indeed.   *(Aſide.*

M E R L I N.

Beware of encroaching a ſingle monoſyllable
upon my injunction ; the moment another word
eſcapes you, you are dumb.

F A T I M A.

Heaven preſerve me ! what will become of
me !

M E R L I N.

Remember what I fay—as you obey or neg-
lect me, you will be punifhed, or rewarded.

[Merlin *ftrikes the fcene, which opens and dif-
covers his dragons and chariot, which carry
him away.*

Farewell *(bowing to her).* Remember me, Fatima.

F A T I M A.

I fhall never forget you, I am fure—What a
polite devil it is—and what a woeful plight am I
in? This confining my tongue to two words is
much worfe than being quite dumb. I had rather be ftinted in any thing than my fpeech—
Heigho—There never fure was a tax upon the
tongue before.

A I R.

Tax my tongue, it is a fhame:
Merlin, fure, is much to blame,
  Not to let it fweetly flow.
Yet the favours of the great,
And the filly maiden's fate,
  Often follow, Yes *or* No.

  Lack-a-day!
  Poor Fatima!
  Stinted fo,
  To Yes *or* No.

II.

Should I want to talk and chat,
Tell Urganda *this or that,*
  How fhall I about it go!

Let

Let her afk me what fhe will,
I muft keep my clapper ftill,
   Striking only Yes *or* No.
      Lack-a-day!
      Poor Fatima!
      Stinted fo,
      To Yes *or* No.   *[Exit.*

S C E N E, *Enter* Cymon *and* Sylvia *(arm
in arm).*

C Y M O N.

You muft not figh, my Sylvia—love like
ours can have no bitter mingled with its fweets.
It has given me eyes, ears, and understanding;
and till they forfake me, I muft be Sylvia's.

S Y L V I A.

And while I retain mine, I know no happinefs but with Cymon ;—and yet Urganda—

C Y M O N

Why will you fully again the purity of our
joys with the thoughts of that unhappy, becaufe
guilty, woman.—Has not Merlin difcovered all
that was unknown to us? Has he not promifed
us his protection, and told us, that we are the
care of fuperior beings, and that more bleffings,
if poffible, are in ftore for us?—What can Sylvia
want, when Cymon is completely bleft?

S Y L V I A.

Nothing but my Cymon ; when that is fecure
to me, I have not a wifh for more.

C Y M O N.

Thy wifhes are fulfilled then, and *mine* in *thee!*
      K 2   SYLVIA.

S Y L V I A.

Take my hand, and with it a heart, which, till you had touch'd, never knew, nor could even imagine, what was love; but my paſſion now is as ſincere as it is tender, and it would be ungrateful to diſguiſe my affections, as they are my greateſt pride and happineſs.

C Y M O.N.

Tranſporting maid !   [*Kiſſes her hand.*

S Y L V I A.

A I R.

This cold flinty heart it is you who have warm'd,
You waken'd my paſſions, my ſenſes have charm'd ;
In vain againſt Merit and Cymon I ſtrove ;
What's life without paſſion—ſweet paſſion of love?

II.

The froſt nips the bud, and the roſe cannot blow,
From youth that is froſt-nipt no raptures can flow,
Elyſium to him but a deſert will prove ;
What's life without paſſion—ſweet paſſion of love ?

III.

The ſpring ſhou'd be warm, the young ſeaſon be gay,
Her birds and her flowrets make blithſome ſweet
     May,
Love bleſſes the cottage, and ſings thro' the grove ;
What's life without paſſion—ſweet paſſion of love ?

C Y M O N.

Thus then I ſeize my treaſure, will protect it with my life, and will never reſign it, but to heaven who gave it me.   [*Embraces her.*

Enter

Enter Damon *and* Dorilas *on one side, and* Dorus *and his followers on the other ; who start at feeing* Cymon *and* Sylvia.

D A M O N.

Here they are !

S Y L V I A.

Ha ! blefs me ! (*ftarting.*)

D O R U S.

Fine doings indeed ;
[*Cymon and* Sylvia *ftand amaz'd and afham'd.*

D O R I L A S.

Your humble fervant, modeft madam Sylvia!

D A M O N.

You are much improv'd by your new tutor.

D O R U S.

But I'll fend her and her tutor where they fhall learn better.—I am confounded at their affurance! Why don't you fpeak, culprits?

C Y M O N.

We may be afham'd without guilt, to be watch'd and furpriz'd by thofe who ought to be more afham'd at what they have done.

S Y L V I A.

Be calm, my Cymon, they mean us mifchief.

C Y M O N.

But they can do us none ;—fear them not, my fhepherdefs.

D O R U S.

Did you ever hear or fee fuch an impudent couple? but I'll fecure you from fuch intemperate doings.

D A M O N.

Shall we feize them, your worfhip, and drag 'em to Urganda?

D O R U S.

Let me fpeak firft with that fhepherdefs.

[As he approaches, Cymon *puts her behind him.*

C Y M O N.

That fhepherdefs is not to be fpoke with.

D O R U S.

Here's impudence in perfection!—Do you know who I am, ftripling?

C Y M O N.

I know you to be one who ought to obferve the laws, and protect innocence; but having paffions that difgrace both your age and place, you neither do one or the other.

D O R U S.

I am aftonifh'd! What are you the foolifh young fellow I have heard fo much of?

C Y M O N.

As fure as you are the wicked old fellow I have heard fo much of.

D O R U S.

Seize them both this inftant.

C Y M O N.

That is fooner faid than done, Governor.

[*As they approach on both fides to feize them, he fnatches a ftaff from one of the fhepherds and beats them back.*]

D O R U S.

Fall on him, but don't kill him, for I muft make an example of him.

C Y M O N.

In this caufe I am myfelf an army; fee how the wretches ftare, and cannot ftir.

A I R.

Come on, come on,
A thoufand to one,
I dare you to come on.
Tho' unpractis'd and young,
Love has made me ftout and ftrong;
Has given me a charm,
Will not fuffer me to fall;
Has fteel'd my heart, and nerv'd my arm,
To guard my precious all.

[*Looking at* Sylvia.
Come on, come on, &c.   [*Exit.*

S Y L V I A.

O Merlin, *now befriend him!*
From their rage defend him!

[*While* Cymon *drives off the party of fhepherds on one fide, enter* Dorus *and his party, who furround* Sylvia.]

D O R U S.

Away with her, away with her—

SYLVIA.

S Y L V I A.

Protect me, Merlin!—Cymon! Cymon! where art thou, Cymon?

D O R U S.

Your fool Cymon is too fond of fighting to mind his mistress; away with her to Urganda, away with her.

[*They hurry her off.*

Enter Shepherds, running across disordered and beaten by Cymon.

Damon (*looking back.*)

'Tis the devil of a fellow! how he has laid about him!

[*Exit.*

D O R I L A S.

There is no way but this to avoid him.

[*Exit.*

Enter Cymon (*in confusion and out of breath.*)

I have conquered, my Sylvia!—Where art thou?—my life, my love, my valour, my all!— What, gone!—torn from me!—then I am con- quer'd, indeed!

[*He runs off, and returns several times during the symphony of the following song.*]

A I R.

A I R.

Torn from me, torn from me, which way did they
*   take her?*
* To death they shall bear me,*
* To pieces shall tear me,*
Before I'll forsake her!
*   Tho' fast bound in a spell,*
*   By* Urganda *and hell,*
*   I'll burst thro' their charms,*
*   Seize my fair in my arms;*
*   Then my valour shall prove,*
No magick like virtue, like Virtue *and* Love *!*

END *of the* FOURTH ACT.

A C T V.

SCENE, *a Grotto.*

Enter URGANDA *and* FATIMA.

URGANDA.

YES!—No!—forbear this mockery—What can it mean?—I will not bear this trifling with my paſſion—Fatima, my heart's upon the rack, and muſt not be ſported with——Let me know the worſt, and quickly—to conceal it from me is not kindneſs, but the height of cruelty—Why don't you ſpeak? (*Fatima ſhakes her head.* Won't you ſpeak?

FATIMA.

Yes.

URGANDA.

Go on then.

FATIMA.

No.

URGANDA.

Will you ſay nothing but No?

FATIMA.

Yes.

U R G A N D A.

Diftracting, treacherous Fatima!—Have you feen my rival?

F A T I M A.

Yes.

U R G A N D A.

Thanks, dear Fatima!—well—now go on.

F A T I M A.

No.

U R G A N D A.

This is not to be born—Was Cymon with her?

F A T I M A.

Yes.

U R G A N D A.

Are they in love with each other?

F A T I M A.

Yes. (*fighing.*)

U R G A N D A.

Where did you fee my rival? (Fatima *fhakes her head.*) Falfe, unkind, obftinate Fatima!—— Won't you tell me?

F A T I M A.

No.

U R G A N D A.

You are brib'd to betray me?

F A T I M A.

No.

U R G A N D A.

What, ftill Yes and No?

FATIMA.

FATIMA.

Yes.

URGANDA.

And not a single word more?

FATIMA.

No.

URGANDA.

Are you afraid of any body?

FATIMA.

Yes.

URGANDA.

Are you not afraid of me too?

FATIMA.

No.

URGANDA.

Infolence! Is my rival handfome? tell me
that.

FATIMA.

Yes.

URGANDA.

Very handfome?

FATIMA.

Yes, yes.

URGANDA.

How handfome? handfomer than I, or you?

FATIMA.

Yes—No—(*hefitating.*)

URGAN-

URGANDA.

How can you fee me thus miferable, and not relieve me? have you no pity for me?

FATIMA.

Yes! (*fighing.*)

URGANDA.

Convince me of it, and tell me all.

FATIMA.

No! (*fighing.*)

URGANDA.

I fhall go diftracted!—Leave me.

FATIMA.

Yes.

URGANDA.

And dare not come into my prefence.

FATIMA.

No.   (*Curtfies, and Exit.*)

Urganda *alone.*

She has a fpell upon her, or fhe could not do thus—Merlin's power has prevailed—he has inchanted her, and my love and my revenge are equally difappointed.—This is the completion of my mifery?

Enter DORUS.

DORUS.

May I prefume to intrude upon my fovereign's contemplations?

URGANDA.

U R G A N D A.

Dare not to approach my mifery, or thou fhalt partake of it.

D O R U S.

I am gone—and Sylvia fhall go too. *(Going.)*

U R G A N D A.

Sylvia, faid you? where is fhe? where is fhe? Speak, fpeak—and give me life or death.

D O R U S.

She is without, and attends your mighty will.

U R G A N D A.

Then I am queen again!—Forgive me, Dorus—I was loft in thought, funk in defpair; I knew not what I faid—but now I am rais'd again!—Sylvia is fafe!

D O R U S.

Yes; and I am fafe too, which is no fmall comfort to me, confidering where I have been.

U R G A N D A.

And Cymon—has he efcap'd?

D O R U S.

Yes, he has efcap'd from us; and, what is better, we have efcap'd from him.

U R G A N D A.

Where is he?

D O R U S.

Breaking the bones of every fhepherd he meets.

U R G A N D A.

Well, no matter—I am in poſſeſſion of the preſent object of my paſſion, and I will indulge it to the height of luxury!—Let 'em prepare my victim inſtantly for death.—

D O R U S.

For death!—Is not that going too far?

U R G A N D A.

Nothing is too far—ſhe makes me ſuffer ten thouſand deaths, and nothing but her's can ap- peaſe me. (Dorus going.) Stay, Dorus—I have a richer revenge; ſhe ſhall be ſhut up in the Black Tower 'till her beauties are deſtroy'd, and then I will preſent her to this ungrateful Cymon— Let her be brought before me, and I will feaſt my eyes, and eaſe my heart, with this devoted Sylvia—No reply, but obey.

D O R U S.

It is done—This is going too far.   [*Aſide.*
          [*Exit, ſhrugging up his ſhoulders.*

Urganda.

Tho' ſtill of raging winds the ſport,
My ſhipwreck'd heart ſhall gain the port;
  Revenge, the pilot, ſteers her way;
No more of tenderneſs and love,
The eagle in her gripe has ſeiz'd the dove,
  And thinks of nothing but her prey.

Enter Sylvia, Dorus, *and* Guards.

U R G A N D A.

Are you the wretch, the unhappy maid, who has dar'd to be the rival of Urganda?

SYLVIA.

S Y L V I A.

I am no wretch, but the happy maid, who am possess'd of the affections of Cymon, and with them have nothing to hope or fear.

U R G A N D A.

Thou vain rash creature!—I will make thee fear my power, and hope for my mercy.
[*Waves her wand, and the scene changes to the Black Rocks.*

S Y L V I A.

I am still unmov'd.   (*Smiling.*)

U R G A N D A.

Thou art on the very brink of perdition, and in a moment wilt be closed in a tower, where thou shalt never see Cymon, or any human being more.

S Y L V I A.

While I have Cymon in my heart, I bear a charm about me, to scorn your power, or, what is more, your cruelty.

[Urganda *waves her wand, and the Black Tower appears.*]

U R G A N D A.

Open the gates, and inclose her insolence for ever.

S Y L V I A.

I am ready.   (*Smiling at* Urganda.)

A I R.

Tho' varicus deaths surround me,
No terrors can confound me ;
Protected from above,
I glory in my love !

Against

Against thy cruel might,
  And in this dreadful hour,
I have a sure defence,
  'Tis innocence!
That heav'nly right,
  To smile on guilty power!

U R G A N D A.

Let me no more be tormented with her; I cannot bear to hear or see her.—Close her in the tower for ever! [*They put* Sylvia *in the tower.*] Now let Merlin release you if he can. [*Exultingly.*

[*It thunders; the tower and rocks give way to a magnificent amphitheatre, and* Merlin *appears in the place where the tower sunk: All shriek, and run off except* Urganda, *who is struck with terror.*]

M E R L I N.

Still shall my power your arts confound ;
And Cymon's *cure shall be* Urganda's *wound.*
                    [Urganda *waves her wand,*

M E R L I N.

Ha! ha! ha!—your power is gone—

U R G A N D A.

I am all terror and shame—in vain I wave this wand—I feel my power is gone, yet I still retain my passions—My misery is complete!

M E R L I N.

It is indeed! No power, no happiness were superior to thine till you sunk them into your folly —you now find, but too late, that there is no magic like virtue. [*Sound of warlike instruments,*

U R G A N D A.

What mean thofe founds of joy?—my heart
forebodes, that they proclaim my fall and dif-
honour.

M E R L I N.

The knights of the different orders of chivalry,
who where fent by *Cymon*'s father in queft of his fon,
were drawn hither, by my power, from their fe-
veral ftations to one fpot, and at the fame inftant :
the general aftonifhment at their meeting, was foon
changed into general joy, when they were told, by
what means, and upon what occafion they were fo
unexpectedly affembled ; and they are now pre-
paring to celebrate and protect the marriage of
Cymon with *Sylvia*.

U R G A N D A.

Death to my hopes!—then I am loft indeed !

M E R L I N.

From the moment you wrong'd me, and
yourfelf, I became their protector—I counter-
acted all your fchemes, I continued Cymon in
his ftate of ignorance till he was cured by Sylvia, whom I conveyed here for that purpofe ;
that fhepherdefs is a princefs equal to Cymon—
They have obtained by their virtues the throne of
Arcadia, which you have loft by——But I have
done; I fee your repentance, and my anger
melts into pity.

U R G A N D A.

Pity me not—I am undeferving of it—I have
been cruel and faithlefs, and ought to be wretched—Thus I deftroy the fmall remains of my fo-
vereignty. (*Breaks her wand.*) May power, bafely
exerted, be ever thus broken and difperfed !
[*Throws away her wand.*

            Forgive

Forgive my errors and forget my name,
O drive me hence with penitence and shame;
From Merlin, Cymon, Sylvia, let me fly,
Beholding them, my shame can never die.

[*Exit* Urganda.

M E R L I N.

Falsehood is punished, virtue rewarded, and
Arcadia is happy!

M A R C H.

[Enter the procession of knights of the different
orders of *Chivalry*, with *Inchanters, &c.* who
range themselves round the amphitheatre, fol-
lowed by *Cymon, Sylvia,* and *Merlin,* who
are brought in triumph drawn by *Loves,* pre-
ceded by *Cupid* and *Hymen* walking arm in
arm. Then enter the *Arcadian* shepherds,
with *Dorus* and *Linco* at their head, *Damon*
and *Dorilas,* with their shepherdesses, *&c.*
Merlin, Cymon and *Sylvia* descend from the car.
Merlin joins their hands, and then speaks the
following lines.]

M E R L I N.

Now join your hands, whose hearts were join'd
before,
This union shall *Arcadia's* peace restore:
When Virtues such as these adorn a throne;
The people make their sovereign's bliss their own:
Their joys, their virtues, shall each subject share;
And all the land reflect the royal pair!

C H O R U S.

Each heart and each voice
In Arcadia *rejoice;*

Let gratitude raise
To great Merlin *our praise :*
Long, long may we share
The blessings of this pair !
Long, long may they live,
To share the bliss they give !

Cymon, Sylvia, *and* Merlin *retire to the knights,
while* Linco *calls the shepherds about him.*

L I N C O.

My good neighbours and friends (for now I am not asham'd to call you so) your deputy Linco has but a short charge to give you.—As we have turn'd over a new, fair leaf, let us never look back to our past blots and errors.

D O R U S.

No more we will, Linco.—No retrospection.

L I N C O.

I meant to oblige your worship in the proposition; I shall ever be a good subject (*bowing to* Cymon *and* Sylvia), and your friend and obedient deputy. Let us have a hundred marriages directly, and no more inconstancy, jealousy, or coquetry from this day.—The best purifier of the blood is mirth, with a few grains of wisdom— we will take it every day, neighbours, as the best preservative against bad humours : *Be merry and wise*, according to the old proverb, and I defy the devil ever to get among you again;—and that we may be sure to get rid of him, let us drive him quite away with a little more singing and dancing, for he hates mortally mirth and good fellowship.

A DANCE

A D A N C E *of* Arcadian *Shepherds and Shepherdesses.*

A I R.

D A M O N.

Each shepherd again shall be constant and kind,
And ev'ry stray'd heart shall each shepherdess find.

D E L I A.

If faithful our shepherds, we always are true,
Our truth and our falshood we borrow from you.

C H O R U S.

Happy Arcadians *still shall be;*
Ever be happy while virtuous and free.

F A T I M A.

Let those who the sword and the balance must hold,
To interest be blind, and to beauty be cold:
When justice has eyes her integrity fails,
Her sword becomes blunted, and down drop her
scales.

C H O R U S.

Happy Arcadians *still shall be;*
Ever be happy while virtuous and free.

L I N C O.

The bliss of your heart no rude care shall molest,
While innocent mirth is your bosom's sweet guest;
Of that happy pair let us worthy be seen,
Love, honour, and copy your king and your queen.

C H O R U S.

CHORUS.

Happy Arcadians *still shall be* ;
Ever be happy while virtuous and free.

SYLVIA.

Let love, peace, and joy still be seen hand in hand,
To dance on this turf, and again bless the land.

CYMON.

Love and Hymen of blessings have open'd their store,
For Cymon *with* Sylvia *can wish nothing more.*

BOTH.

Love and Hymen of blessings have open'd their store,

HE.

For Cymon *with* Sylvia

SHE.

For Sylvia *with* Cymon

} can wish nothing more.

CHORUS.

Happy Arcadians *still shall be* ;
Ever be happy while virtuous and free.

F I N I S.

EPILOGUE,

Written by GEORGE KEATE, Efq.

Spoken by Mrs. ABINGTON.

Enter, peeping in at the Stage-Door.

IS the ftage clear?—blefs me!—I've fuch a dread!
It feems enchanted ground, where'er I tread!
　　　　　　　　　　　[Coming forward.
What noife was that!—hufh!—'twas a falfe alarm—
I'm fure there's no one here will do me harm:
Among'ft you can't be found a fingle knight,
Who would not do an injur'd damfel right.
Well—Heav'n be prais'd! I'm out of magic reach,
And have once more regain'd the pow'r of fpeech:
Aye, and I'll ufe it—for it muft appear,
That my poor tongue is greatly in arrear——
There's not a female here but fhar'd my woe,
Ty'd down to YES, or ftill more hateful NO.
NO is expreffive—but I muft confefs,
If rightly queftion'd, I'd ufe only YES.
　　In MERLIN's walk this broken wand I found,
　　　　　　[Shewing a broken wand.
Which to *two Words* my fpeaking organs bound.
Suppofe upon the town I try his fpell——
Ladies, don't ftir!—You ufe your tongues too well!
How tranquil every place, when, by my fkill,
Folly is mute, and even *Slander* ftill!
Old Goffips fpeechlefs—*Bloods* would breed no riot,
And all the tongues at *Jonathan's* lie quiet!
Each *grave Profeffion* muft new bufh the wig;
Nothing to fay, 'twere needlefs they look big!
The *reverend Doctor* might the change endure,
He would fit ftill, and have his *Sine Cure!*
Nor could *Great Folks* much hardfhip undergo;
They do their bus'nefs with an AYE or NO!—
But, come, I only jok'd—difmifs your fear;
Tho' I've the pow'r, I will not ufe it here.

　　　　　　　　　　　　　　　　　　I'll

E P I L O G U E.

I'll only keep my magic as a guard,
To awe each critic who attacks our bard.
I see some malcontents their fingers biting,
Snarling, " The ancients never knew such writing—
" The drama's loft!—the managers exhauft us
" With *Op'ras, Monkies, Mab,* and *Dr. Fauftus.*"
Dread Sirs, a word !—the public tafte is fickle ;
All palates in their turn we ftrive to tickle.
Our cat'rers *vary* ; and you'll own, at leaft,
It is *Variety* that makes the feaft.
If this fair circle fmile—and *the Gods* thunder,
I with this wand will keep the critics under.